# The Night Fairy

# The Night Fairy

## Laura Amy Schlitz

illustrated by
Angela Barrett

WALKER
BOOKS

First published in Great Britain 2011 by Walker Books Ltd
87 Vauxhall Walk, London SE11 5HJ

2 4 6 8 10 9 7 5 3 1

Text © 2010 Laura Amy Schlitz
Illustrations © 2010 Angela Barrett

This book has been typeset in Veljovic

Printed in China

British Library Cataloguing in Publication Data: a catalogue
record for this book is available from the British Library

ISBN 978-1-4063-3138-7

www.walker.co.uk

This one is for Mary Lee,

*sine qua non.*

*L. A. S.*

Chapter One
*Flory*

Flory was a night fairy. She was born a little before midnight when the moon was full. For the rest of her life—and fairies can live hundreds of years—that hour, a little before midnight, would be the time when her magic was strongest.

Flory was at home in the dark. Like all night fairies, she cast a silver shadow, which helped her to hide in the moonlight. She had great sharp eyes that sparkled like blackberries under dew, and a tangle of dusky curls.

Her wings had thin feathers at the tips. These were her sensing feathers. If there was a mouse nearby, Flory felt its body heat through her feathers. If it was about to rain, her feathers felt the water in the air.

Flory was proud of her wings. Night fairies, like moths, often have drab wings, but Flory's were pale green with amber moons on them. These wings were the cause of Flory's great trouble.

There are those who say that fairies have no troubles, but this is not true. Fairies are magical creatures, but they can be hurt—even killed—when they are young and their magic is not strong. Young fairies have no one to take care of them, because fairies make bad parents. Babies bore them. A fairy godmother is an excellent thing, but a fairy mother is a disaster.

Because fairies do not look after their children, young fairies have to take care of themselves. Luckily, they can walk and talk as soon as they are born. After three days, they will not drink milk and have no more use for their mothers. They drink dew and suck the nectar from flowers. On the seventh day of life, their wings unfold, and they fly away from home.

On the night of Flory's peril, she was less than three months old. It was a windy night: cool and sweet with springtime. Flory was coasting on the breeze, letting it toss her wherever it liked. She was still very tiny—as tall as an acorn—and her green wings glittered in the moonlight. A little brown bat swooped down upon her, caught her, and crunched up her wings.

Flory cried out. If she had been a little bit older, she might have shouted a spell to sting the bat's mouth. If she had been a hundred years old, she could have cast a spell to make her wings grow back in an instant. But the cry

that came from her was no spell at all, only a sound of pain and loss.

The little bat, realizing his mistake, opened his mouth and spat. He stammered, "So sorry!" but Flory did not hear. There was blood on her wings, and she was falling through the night, spinning like a maple seed.

She landed on the branch of a cherry tree. She grabbed hold of a clump of white blossoms and clung to them, shaking. Never before had she known pain. For the first time in her life, her eyes filled with tears, but she did not cry. She knew she must think what to do next.

She peered through the blossoms. Three trees stood together: the cherry tree, a thorn apple, and an oak. They were not wild trees. Flory had been born in the woods, and she knew at once that a giant had planted them—a stupid giant, who had not given them room to grow. She had fallen into a giant's garden.

Flory turned, gazing all around. The garden

was surrounded by a high wooden fence. At one end was a fishpond with a fountain, and a brick patio with an iron table and two chairs. Beyond the patio stood a huge house made of bricks.

Flory let go of the cherry blossoms and ran her hand up her back, trying to feel what was left of her wings. All but one of her sensing feathers had been bitten off. There was a double ruffle of wings going up her spine, but it was narrow: only as wide as her hand. She knew at once she would not be able to fly. Flory's mouth opened and a great sob came out.

The sound frightened her. Bats have keen hearing. Now that she had no wings, she must be careful not to call attention to herself. The night was full of hungry creatures: bats, owls, even the crawling snakes. She gazed up and down the tree trunk. Perhaps she could find a crack in the bark where she could hide.

But the cherry was a young tree, and its

bark was smooth. The nearby oak was riddled with holes, but they were big hollows that might be homes for bats. At the thought of bats, her blood ran cold.

All at once, her eyes fixed on a strange shape. Dangling from the limb of the cherry tree was a little box made of wood. One side had a peg sticking out and a door hole the size of a small dandelion. Flory did not know giants well enough to know that they sometimes made houses for birds and hung them in the trees.

Flory stared at the box, head cocked. She sensed that it was empty. It would make a good hiding place: not too small, but not too big. No bat would be able to fit its wings through the door. A twig grew close to the little box. She darted to the end of the twig, clasped her hands around it, and swung downward, feeling with her feet for the wooden peg. When her toes touched it, she stood, balancing like an acrobat.

The box smelled of cedar, which was good—Flory was fussy about smells. The words *A Souvenir from Niagara Falls* were written in a half-moon over the door hole. Flory could not read, but she liked the picture underneath: a blue waterfall surrounded by rainbows. She climbed up, perching on the edge of the door hole. Then she hopped down.

Inside it was pitch-dark, but Flory's eyes were made for the night, and she had no trouble seeing. The floor was littered with twigs, left over from a time when the house held wrens. Flory shoved the twigs into one corner.

All at once she was so tired that her knees felt weak. She knelt down and curled up on her side—fairies do not sleep on their backs because of their wings—and thought about warm things: the breast feathers of a bird, the softness of a mulberry leaf, the nubbins of pussy willow. As she thought of them, her tiny body stopped shivering, and she fell asleep.

## Chapter Two
# Daylight

Flory slept in the wren house all the next day. When night came, she was awakened by thirst. Her wings ached, and her stomach growled. Trembling, she got to her feet and went to the door.

She stood by the door hole for a long time. Outside the cedar house, the creatures of the night searched for prey. The squeak of a faraway bat made her shiver. Hugging herself, she crept back to her place beside the twigs.

When she woke again, it was morning. Just

as a human person may wake in the middle of the night, a night fairy, if greatly troubled, may wake during the day. Flory blinked. She had never seen anything as blue as the sky outside her door hole.

She staggered to the door. The morning light made her head throb.

The cedar house overlooked a flower bed. A giant—from the smell, it was a giantess—had planted tulips there. They were vast balloons of color: butter yellow, blood red, pink with green stripes. The fountain was splashing in the sunlight, and the water was frothy with bubbles and alive with gaudy orange fish.

The brilliance of the garden made Flory rub her eyes. All the same, the colors thrilled her, making her heart race and her skin tingle. For a moment she forgot the pain of her broken wings. She pulled herself up to sit in the doorway, feet dangling. The wind ruffled the cherry blossoms above her head. She pulled a cluster of petals nearer and drank the dew off them. Then she gorged herself on pollen, ripping handfuls from the blossoms.

After she had eaten her fill, she sat and gazed at the garden. There were no bats in sight: only butterflies—but they were no danger—and birds. Flory had never seen such noisy and energetic birds. They swooped and lunged from branch to branch, twittering and caroling and swearing at the tops of their lungs. All of them looked huge to Flory, but she knew that most of them ate seeds or small insects, not fairies. She wished she were a day fairy and could live in a world with birds instead of bats.

An idea flew into her head. Flory sat up straight and raised her chin.

"From now on," she said firmly, "I will be a day fairy."

Being a day fairy was not easy. Flory had never met a day fairy, and she knew little about their lives. Day fairies are afraid of giants, and they live in the wild places in the world. Night fairies, on the other hand, have a daredevil streak; they like to see how close they can come to giants without being seen. Even the boldest fairy would not choose to live in a giant's garden, but Flory had no choice. Without wings, she couldn't escape, and she needed the shelter of the cedar house.

She soon found that her body did not like the day. Her skin liked to be cool and moist, not hot and dry. When the shadows fell, her whole body itched with alertness, and she found it hard to sleep. Sunshine made her eyes water, which made her irritable. It is always prettier when fairies are not irritable, but Flory could not help herself. She missed her wings, and she had to make a whole new life for herself, with no one to show her how.

She hauled the twigs out of the wren house and covered the floor with cherry blossoms,

13

casting a spell over them so they wouldn't wilt. She gathered thin blades of grass and wove them into baskets for the storage of fresh greens. With unskilled hands, she knotted together a dress of cherry blossom so that she could blend in with the flowers on the tree. The day after she finished it, a strong rain came and tore the blossoms away, which made Flory shake her fist at the sky.

She spent a great deal of time sitting on the peg outside her door hole, watching the garden. She noticed that the oak tree drew more birds than any tree in the garden. First one bird, then another, swooped at the tree and darted happily away. When she looked closely, she saw that there was a metal hook in the tree. Dangling from the hook was a clear tube full of seeds. It was this tube that drew the birds. They came to eat the seeds.

Flory shook her head, baffled. Fairies are born knowing certain things, and one of the things she knew was that seeds come from plants, not from round tubes. All the same, the seeds smelled as if they might be good to eat. Just as she was thinking about the best way to climb down the tree, the door of the great house opened, and the giantess came out.

She was—if Flory had known it—a rather small giantess, but she was the largest creature Flory had ever seen. She had white braids that crisscrossed over her head, and woolly slippers on her feet. She lumbered over to the oak tree and filled the tube with fresh seeds.

Flory watched, holding her breath.

The giantess wandered over to the fishpond. She opened a tall can that had pictures of fish on the side, and sprinkled little sticks on the water. The fish came to the surface, gulping and flicking their tails. The giantess watched them, making cheerful noises. After five minutes or so, she waddled back into the house.

Flory thought about the giantess for a long

time. She knew that giants were supposed to be very terrible, but it was hard to be afraid of anything so old and so slow. She reached behind her back to scratch the scabs on her left wing. She had never been taught to be afraid of bats. The bat people and the night fairies had been at peace for a thousand years.

And yet it was a bat, not a giant, who had taken her wings.

"I'm not afraid of giants," Flory boasted aloud. It sounded so daring that she said it again, swinging her feet. "I'm not a bit afraid of giants. But I hate bats."

It was quite safe to say so, because the bats were all asleep.

"I hate bats," Flory repeated, "I hate, hate, *hate* bats, and I'm always going to hate them."

It seemed like a good decision. Flory lolled back against the side of the house, enjoying the fragrance of onion grass and grape hyacinths. She wondered if the grape hyacinths tasted as good as they smelled. Tomorrow she would climb down the tree and find out. It would be a long trip, but she was quick and agile, and she didn't have a lazy bone in her body.

She shaded her eyes with her hand and gazed at the thorn apple tree. She admired its long, sharp thorns. If she could break the thorns off the tree, she might be able to make herself a pocketknife or even a dagger. She liked the idea of a dagger. If a bat ever attacked again, she would take out her dagger and stab it to the heart, and then . . .

Flory dozed. The spring day was warm, and she was dreaming of slaying bats. Suddenly the sensing feather on her left wing stirred. Something was nearby — a warm-blooded animal, a large animal. She leaped to her feet.

The squirrel was only inches away. He was huge, almost twice as big as the flying squirrels she had known: a mountain of shaggy fur and sharp claws. Flory knew he ate almost everything that could be eaten: acorns, nuts, seeds, insects, eggs, baby birds. . . . She saw that his eyes were fixed on her and his nostrils were twitching hungrily.

Fear flashed through her like lightning. Her mouth opened, and she shrieked.

The squirrel leaped aside, startled. In an instant he was halfway down the tree, but Flory went on screaming. "Get away from me!" she shouted. "Don't touch me!" All at once, her mouth was full of words she had never spoken before. As she yelled them, the squirrel jumped straight up in the air as if he had been burned.

"That's right!" Flory cried. "Go away, or I'll sting you again!"

The squirrel tore off across the yard. Flory watched him scramble up the wooden fence and disappear over the top. She put her hands up to her mouth. She was smiling.

"I said a magic spell," she said. She did not know where the words of her spell had come from, but she was overjoyed. "I can take care of myself."

She had discovered a new spell, a stinging spell. Fairies are not taught magic as human children are taught the alphabet. Fairies are born with the seeds of spells in their minds. As they grow older, the spells grow too, like the little white teeth that sprout from a baby's gums. The stinging spell had come to Flory because she was old enough to use it—and because she needed it.

"I like that spell," said Flory. "I'm never going to forget it. I'll practice it over and over—and if I ever see a bat again, I'll sting him until he squeaks."

## Chapter Three

# Skuggle

If a person—whether she is human or fairy—spends most of her time thinking of ways to sting, it is bound to show. In the weeks that followed, Flory practiced her stinging spell so often that she began to have rather a prickly look. Her nose and chin grew more pointed, as did the tips of her ears.

Spring drew closer to summer. The tulips dropped their petals, and the peonies bloomed, fat mattresses of milky petals and rich smells. Flory grew used to the sound of birds singing and the sight of them making their nests. She even grew used to the giantess, who came every day to fill the clear tube with seeds. Flory began to hanker after the seeds herself. She knew that after summer came autumn and then winter. She was not afraid of the cold—a fairy can lie naked in the snow and warm herself with magic—but she thought it might be a good idea to fill her house with food. When winter came, there would be no green shoots and no pollen. She could not fly south like the birds. A little cache of seeds and nuts would be very useful.

She decided to make a rope bridge to the oak tree. She began to gather dried cobwebs, which could be spun into long ropes and knotted into ladders. If she could travel from tree to tree without climbing down to the ground, it would save hours. She would be able to raid the seed tube every day.

Making the rope bridge took time. Even

when dried, the spiderwebs were sticky, and Flory had no knife to cut them; she had to gnaw them with her teeth. The spinning work was hard, too, until she found a spell to help her. She twisted the strings of cobweb together and closed her eyes, thinking of the way a vine twists around a tree branch. After a moment or two, the cobwebs began to writhe like snakes in her lap. Flory breathed steadily, letting her magic flow from her hands to the cobwebs. When at last she opened her eyes, the strands had twirled together, forming a rope that was stronger than steel.

She had just finished a new rope when her sensing feather throbbed. At once she jumped up, ready to sting. The squirrel leaped down through the cherry tree, landing on the roof of Flory's house. Flory was not surprised to see him. He tried to pounce on her at least once a day. By now, he ought to have known that it was no good—Flory always stung him—but he was either very hopeful or very foolish; Flory didn't know which.

The squirrel stood on top of the wooden house, his paws dangling over his white belly. His nose twitched. He looked as if he were trying to make up his mind whether or not to pounce.

"I wouldn't if I were you," Flory said to the squirrel.

The squirrel leaped. Flory spoke the words of her stinging spell almost before he moved. It hit the squirrel in midair. He twisted and shied away from her. "I told you," Flory taunted him.

The squirrel turned tail and dove down the cherry tree. He headed for the seed tube. Flory had noticed that he was very fond of the seed tube. He hung on to it for hours, gobbling seeds.

But today there was a new tube, one with

a clear dome at the top. The birds had to fly under the dome to get the seeds.

The squirrel looked puzzled and then worried. He leaped onto the dome, but it was slippery and his claws had nothing to hold on to. If he clung to the hook and hung upside down, his front paws couldn't reach the food tray. If he let go of the hook, he slid down the dome and landed on the grass. Flory burst out laughing.

She watched for an hour. The squirrel jumped onto the dome again and again, his claws scrabbling for a foothold. He stretched himself, flattening his body. He tried leaping straight up from the ground, but it was no use. There was room for the birds to fly between the dome and the seed tray, but there wasn't room enough for him. Flory laughed heartily, but she began to wish that he would get a little bit of food. In the past weeks, she had learned how hard it was to fend off hunger. She didn't feel sorry for him, exactly. She had never learned how to feel *sorry,* even for herself. But her laughter grew less shrill and her eyes looked rather thoughtful.

At last the squirrel gave up. He streaked over the grass and galloped up the cherry tree. He stopped in his tracks when he saw Flory. His beady eyes glistened. He was truly hungry now.

"Don't," Flory warned him, but the squirrel paid no attention. He flung himself at her, only to give a cry of pain.

"How stupid you are!" Flory said. She didn't know how rude she was; she had never been taught manners. "I've stung you twice already, and I'll sting you every time you try to pounce on me. You can't eat me! I'll hurt you if you try."

The squirrel sat back on his haunches. "I'm not stupid," he said in a muffled voice. "I'm hungry."

"You can be both," Flory pointed out.

The squirrel thought about this. He shook his head. "I can never think on an empty stomach," he said, "and my stomach is always empty."

Flory thought of pointing out that this meant he was always stupid, but she didn't. Looking closely, she could see he was rather a young squirrel. His grizzled coat hung slack, and his tail was skimpy.

"You could still get the seeds from the seed tube," Flory said, "only you're going about it the wrong way. It's a new seed tube. Didn't you notice?"

The squirrel nodded. "The giantess keeps putting up new tubes," he complained, "and each one is harder to get into. I don't understand it. She must want me to eat the seeds, or she wouldn't hang the tube in the tree."

"She's a giantess," Flory said. "You can't expect her to have any sense."

The squirrel cocked his head as if he had just had a new idea. "You're a night fairy," he said. "I can tell from your shadow. Why are you awake in the middle of the day?"

"I'm a day fairy now," Flory said.

"You're supposed to be a night fairy," said the squirrel, "and your wings are all broken off."

Flory frowned. She didn't like to talk about her wings. "What's your name, squirrel?" she asked haughtily.

The squirrel scratched. "I'm hungry," he repeated.

"I'm not going to call you that," Flory said. "I think I'll call you Skuggle. *Skug* is another word for *squirrel*, you know."

"Skuggle," echoed the squirrel. He tried it out. "Hungry Skuggle."

"Listen to me," Flory said briskly. "I can help you get the seeds from the new tube, but I want some seeds for myself." A brilliant idea came into her mind. "And I want to ride on your back."

Skuggle stood with his paws at his sides and stretched his neck upward. It was something he did when he was trying to think. "No. I want to eat *all* the seeds. You can't have any."

"Greedy," Flory jeered. "You can't have them all. But if you do what I tell you, you'll get some. That's better than none."

Skuggle's paws twitched. He had very dainty little paws. They looked like tiny gray gloves. "I want the seeds."

"Then you have to let me ride on your back."

Skuggle shifted his weight from side to side. "You won't weigh much," he said, thinking the matter over, "and I'll get the seeds. It's good."

Flory took a step toward him. He was so big that looking up at him made her neck ache. "You're very wide."

"If you take hold of the end of my tail, I can flick you onto my back," said Skuggle. "Only you have to tell me about the seeds, you know."

"I will," said Flory. "Let me up."

She caught hold of the edge of the squirrel's tail and wrapped her arms and legs around it. The tail lashed forward. In another moment, Flory crawled up the squirrel's neck and settled down beside his right ear.

"Now, listen," she said into the squirrel's ear. "You can't get the seeds from the top. The dome is in the way. And you can't get in from the bottom, either. You won't fit."

"What can I do?" asked Skuggle. He sounded as if he might start to cry.

"You can knock the seeds out of the tube," Flory said. "Go up the oak tree and grab hold of the hook—the *hook*, you hear—because you can hold on to that. Swing back and forth as hard as you can. The seeds will fall out of the tube, and you can eat them off the ground."

Skuggle's eyes glistened with greed and hope. "I love you," he said happily.

## Chapter Four

# The Hummingbird

Flory was no longer alone. She felt that she had made a friend, though she wasn't quite sure what friendship was. Skuggle was not the best of friends, because he would have eaten her if he could; also, he never talked about anything but food. Flory wasn't the best of friends, either. She knew that if she had been able to fly, she wouldn't have bothered with Skuggle. She was using him. All the same, after she struck her bargain with Skuggle, she was less lonely.

She had not known she was lonely before. If she hadn't lost her wings, she would have lived with other fairies. They would have played and danced together, swapping riddles and songs and spells. Other fairies might have taught Flory manners, because fairies simply do not put up with rudeness from their friends. But Skuggle had no manners to teach Flory, and when she was rude to him, he just scratched himself. That was all right with Flory. She enjoyed bickering with him. It was more interesting than talking to herself.

She sometimes wondered how she had managed before she met Skuggle. Perched behind his ear, she explored every inch of the garden. Skuggle took her to the thorn apple tree and gnawed off a long thorn that made her an excellent dagger. In return, Flory helped the squirrel get suet from a little box with a cage around it. The cage had such tiny holes that Skuggle couldn't get his paws inside. Flory reached through the bars with her dagger and scraped off gobs of suet for the hungry squirrel. She soon learned that Skuggle would do anything for suet or seeds.

Skuggle was not easy to ride. He was much too big for Flory, and his stride was so rough that she clung to his ear for dear life. Riding him was like riding a roller coaster: now fast, now slow. Flory never knew when he would tear straight up a tree trunk or leap to another tree. He often forgot where she wanted to go and bounded off after something to eat. Still, it was a great thing to be able to move about quickly. It made Flory realize how much she missed her wings.

She began to study the other creatures of the garden, wondering if any of them might be coaxed into carrying her through the air. The butterflies were tempting, but butterflies are absentminded; when Flory tried to talk to them, they flounced their painted wings and drifted off. The dragonflies were almost as beautiful as the butterflies, and Flory thought they looked clever. But dragonflies are moody and, like bats, fond of eating moths. Flory didn't think she could trust them.

There remained the birds. By now, Flory knew the birds of the garden very well. She liked the chickadees and the titmice but avoided the meat eaters: the blue jays, the grackles, and the crows. She admired the scarlet crest of the cardinal and the yellow feathers of the goldfinch. Watching the birds fly brought a lump into Flory's throat. She missed flying dreadfully.

Flory saw her perfect mount one morning in June. She heard a whirring noise and saw a shimmer in the air—a dark patch only a little larger than a bee. Then the creature caught the light. He was a hummingbird. His feathers were emerald green and glittered like mica. His throat was reddish purple, fiery hot one second, cool violet the next. He hovered beside an orange lily. His wings whirred so fast that Flory couldn't see them.

"Oh," whispered Flory. She was filled with such wonder that she could not speak. Her skin was prickly with gooseflesh. It wasn't until he darted away that she remembered to breathe. Then she leaped to her feet and raced to the very tip of the cherry branch. Oh, he was gone! But he would come back, and when he did, she would talk to him. She would tell him how much she wanted him—needed him. He was the most beautiful, most magical creature she had ever seen. And he was just the right size for her: large enough to carry her easily, but small enough so that she could wrap her legs around his neck.

She was sure she could tame him. The thought made her want to leap in the air and shout with joy. She would tame him and make

him her own. Someday—Flory was sure of it—she would straddle his ruby-red throat and soar above the flowers. He would be hers, her very own, and he would take her wherever she liked.

Chapter Five

*Ignored*

Three days after Flory saw the humming-bird, the giantess hung another tube from the oak tree.

Flory squinted. It was almost sunset and she was looking west, but she could see that the new tube was filled with liquid, not seeds. The bottom of the tube had red metal daisies on it. Flory thought this queer: daisies are white, not red, and no flower is made of metal. She cupped her hands around her mouth.

"Skug! Skug! Skuggle!"

The boughs of the thorn apple trembled. Down the tree came Skuggle, lashing his tail with excitement. He spurted over the grass, surged up the cherry tree, and arrived at Flory's side in a rush that made her feather tip shake.

"Is there something to eat?"

Flory pointed to the tube. "I don't know. The giantess put that out, but I don't know what's in it."

Skuggle scratched behind his ear. "Oh, that. She put that out last year. It's mostly water." He looked down at his claw, saw that there was a flea clinging to the tip, and poked the flea into his mouth. "I got on it last year. It's a little slippery, but I can catch hold. The only thing is, it's not worth the trouble. It's just water and some sweet."

"I can't think why she puts out those things."

"That's easy." Skuggle scratched his other

ear. "She wants to eat us. She puts food out so we'll come for it. Then she can kill us."

"Yes, but she never does kill us."

Skuggle bobbed his head, agreeing. "That's because we're too quick for her. But if we didn't run away, she would eat us."

"She must be a great fool."

"Oh, yes," agreed Skuggle. "Only Chickadee says—" He snatched a ripe cherry off the tree and crammed it into his mouth.

"What does the chickadee say?" asked Flory. She had noticed that the chickadee was one of the boldest birds in the yard. He sometimes ate from the seed tube when the giantess was sitting on the patio.

"Chickadee says she doesn't hate us. Chickadee says the giantess puts out seed because she likes us. But Chickadee is wrong, because the giantess eats birds. Big birds. I've seen the bones in the garbage."

Flory wrinkled her nose. Before she had lived near giants, she hadn't known about garbage. The giantess kept a big green can of it in the yard. Raccoons sometimes broke in at night and strewed the garbage over the lawn. Skuggle knew better than to fight the raccoons for something to eat—they were much bigger and stronger than he was—but he feasted on garbage the following mornings, when the raccoons slept. He always smelled awful after eating garbage. Flory tried to shame him by pinching her nostrils shut and looking prim, but Skuggle didn't care. It was almost impossible to make Skuggle feel bad when his stomach was full.

"You should keep away from that garbage," Flory warned him. "Last time you ate yourself sick."

"Oh, dear, yes," sighed Skuggle, "how good that was!" He glanced back at the water tube.

"Why do you want to know about that tube? That's not for us. It's for hummingbirds. They like to suck on the fake flowers."

"Do they?" asked Flory. "In that case, I want to go there—to the oak tree."

"I thought you didn't like that tree late in the day. There's bats in that tree," Skuggle reminded her. "You're frightened of bats."

Flory knew it. A colony of bats nestled in the hollow at the top of the tree. Often she heard them squeaking in the garden after dark. She stuffed her ears with cobwebs in order to block out the sound, but she had bad dreams all the same. "The bats won't be out till dusk," she said. "Anyway, I'm not frightened of them. I just happen to hate them. It's not the same thing."

Skuggle looked sly. "You hate them because you're afraid of them," he said. He lowered his voice and sang a little song. "Fraidy-cat," he sang softly. "Fraidy-cat! Flory-dory fraidy-cat!"

"If you don't stop that, I'll sting you," Flory said coldly.

Skuggle shut his mouth and looked meek.

"Turn around so I can climb on your tail. I want to go to the oak tree."

"Why?" demanded Skuggle.

"So that I can talk to the hummingbirds. Take me there now, and I'll spear some suet for you later."

"Why don't you give it to me now?"

"Because I won't. I'll feed you later, but not now."

Skuggle turned his tail in her direction. "I don't see what you want with hummingbirds. They're nasty birds," he warned her. "I went to rob a nest once, and the mother nearly pecked my eye out. And the eggs were tiny," he added petulantly. "Not much bigger than peas. Hardly worth eating."

Flory paid no attention. She climbed onto the squirrel's tail and waited for him to flick her onto his ear. In another moment, Skuggle leaped from the cherry tree to the oak tree. He stopped by the tube with the metal flowers. Flory slid off. "You can go now," she said, and Skuggle dashed off again.

Flory waited for a long time. As she waited, she imagined the hummingbird again: the magic of his feathers in the light, the rapid double circles he made with his wings. She tried to imagine what it must be like to fly with wings like that. She lifted her arms, muscles tight, and fluttered the edges of her fingers. She imagined wings quivering, drumming on the air.

All at once the drumming sound was real. The hummingbird hovered beside the water tube. He was so close that Flory could feel the wind of his flight. His feathers rippled like green water; his wings were shadow and speed.

"Hummingbird!" cried Flory. "I want you!"

The hummingbird dug his beak into the metal flower. After sucking at the water tube, he darted backward and rose straight into the air. He did not pay one bit of attention to Flory.

"Hummingbird, come back!" shouted Flory.

But he did not come back until he was thirsty again. Flory began to visit the feeder every day, waiting for him to appear. She soon found out that there were four hummingbirds that used the feeder: three males and a female. They drank the sugar water fiercely, as if they had a raging thirst. They were fierce, too, in the way they fought over the feeder, stabbing with their sharp beaks like swordsmen. Flory liked their fierceness. She would not have liked them half as much if they had been tame. She liked the males best, because of the ruby-colored patch on their throats, but she would have happily taken a female bird for her mount. Male or female, the hummingbirds had one thing in common: they ignored Flory as if she were invisible. Again and again she called out to them. Not one of them bothered to look her way.

"Nasty things," Flory said, echoing Skuggle. But she didn't mean it. She still wanted a hummingbird of her own—wanted one dreadfully—and when she dreamed at night, it was of sitting astride that jewel-green back, floating over a wilderness of flowers.

Chapter Six
*Trapped!*

🌿 Midsummer came, a season of blinding-hot days and evening thunderstorms. Flory disliked the heat of the sun, but she enjoyed the storms, especially when they came at night. She liked to think of the bats getting wet.

Flory was growing up. She was as tall as two acorns now, and her curls brushed her shoulders. She could climb as nimbly as an insect, and leap from twig to twig as recklessly as Skuggle himself. Her little house was full of things she had made: a lily-leaf hammock, a quilt of woven grass, and a score of airy gowns crafted from poppies and rose petals. She had food saved for the winter: a mound of sunflower seeds and three snapdragon flowers stuffed with pollen.

She spent a week harvesting cherries, hacking them apart with her dagger, cutting out the pits, and drying them with a magic spell. Every day she learned new spells. They came into her head like songs.

She was half-asleep beside the humming-bird feeder one afternoon when she heard a blue jay squawking. At first she ignored him, because she knew how much blue jays enjoy making noise. They like to take a scrap of song or a piece of news and repeat it over and over, just for the thrill of screaming. But though they shriek for the fun of it, they often tell the truth about what is going on. And this blue jay was shrieking "hummingbird" and "spiderweb" and "trapped!"

Flory sat bolt upright. She peered around the garden without seeing either the hummingbird or the spiderweb. She opened her mouth to shout for Skuggle, and then shut it. Skuggle had been known to eat baby birds. If the hummingbird was caught in a spiderweb, Skuggle might eat him.

An idea took shape in her mind. She shut her eyes and pressed the palms of her hands against her eyelids. She half hissed, half prayed, "Let me see the hummingbird!"

It was a new magic, one she had never tried. At first she saw only the reddish glow of her inner eyelids. Then she saw the spiderweb. It belonged to the black-and-yellow spider that patrolled the juniper bush by the side gate. The sticky threads had snared the hummingbird's wings. The more the bird struggled, the more it was held fast.

"I'll come," Flory said breathlessly. "Don't be afraid, hummingbird! I'll save you!"

She looked down, saw a twig below her, and leaped for it. Once she caught hold, she looked below for another. It was a haphazard, dangerous way to get to the ground, but she had no time to waste. She flung herself from twig to twig until she reached the bottom branch. Then she shinnied down the trunk.

Blades of grass rustled like cornstalks over her head. Flory wished she had thought to bring her dagger so that she could cut her way through the tangles. The idea crossed her mind that she had no idea how she was going to save the bird. Still, she had her magic, and her mind was made up. It would have to be enough.

She thrashed through the grass, breaking into a run when she came to the open space of the patio. By the time she reached the side gate, she was out of breath. She saw the spiderweb above her—a great silver network covering

most of the juniper bush. The trapped bird was less than a foot from the ground.

"I'm coming!" shouted Flory. "Don't be frightened! I'm coming to save you, hummingbird!"

Once the words were out, she clapped her hand over her mouth. Web-building spiders do not stray far from their webs: the spider must be close at hand. But by a stroke of good luck, the spider was nowhere to be seen. Perhaps she was busy with other prey. All the same, she might return at any moment.

Flory jumped straight up into the air, catching the bottom branch of the juniper bush. She swung back and forth until she hooked her legs over the branch. "I've come to set you free," she said breathlessly. "I'm going to pull the web off you. Only you must promise me something first."

The hummingbird twisted its head to look

at her. The feathers under its chin were pearly white. It was a female.

"I've seen you," said Flory. "You come to the water feeder."

"I've never seen *you*," said the hummingbird. She craned her head for another look. "Why are you awake? You're a night fairy."

"I used to be a night fairy," Flory said. "Now I'm not. Will you promise?"

"Promise?" asked the hummingbird.

"Yes," said Flory. She felt her cheeks grow warm; she was not often ashamed, but she felt a little awkward about what she was going to say. She took a deep breath and spoke very clearly so that she wouldn't have to say it twice. "I'll set you free, but after I set you free, you must be my very own hummingbird and let me ride on your back."

She waited for the hummingbird to agree, but the hummingbird was still. The glittering wings were motionless. When they didn't catch the light, they were plain gray. Flory gave a nervous little laugh.

"No," said the hummingbird.

"No?" echoed Flory.

"No," said the hummingbird. "I won't belong to you. I belong to myself. And I have eggs." A note of pride came into her voice. "If I get free, I shall have to look after my nestlings. I shan't have time to bother with you."

Flory could not think what to say next. She reached upward, pulling herself closer to the bird. "But I *want* to cut you free," she said. "I'd like to. If you don't get free, you'll die."

The hummingbird's throat moved. Her beak was open; she was panting for breath. "If I die, the eggs will die," she said hoarsely. "Night will fall, and it will be cold—and the chicks will die inside the shells."

Flory felt a funny ache in her throat. She

was not the kind of fairy who cried easily, and she didn't think the hummingbird cried at all. But the words "the chicks will die" made her feel queer, as if her heart were swollen and sore. She gave herself a little shake, trying to replace the queer feeling with crossness. "It's your own fault," she said. "I'm perfectly willing to set you free. All you have to do is promise to be mine. Then you can warm the eggs, and the chicks won't die."

"I can't promise," said the hummingbird.

"Why not?" demanded Flory.

"Because I can't lie. Hummingbirds don't."

Flory inched closer. "I wouldn't make you serve me all the time," she coaxed. "Only sometimes. I want to ride on your back."

"It doesn't matter what you want," said the hummingbird in her low, scratchy voice. "I can't think about that. My eggs are growing cold."

Flory glowered at the hummingbird. All at once, she wanted to burst into tears. She wanted to stamp her feet and shout and kick. She realized that she was going to free the hummingbird and get nothing in return.

"Hold still," she said furiously. "I'm going to set you free. You don't deserve it, but I'm going to help."

She yanked one of the strands in the web. But the web would not break. Instead, it stretched. When Flory tried to jerk away, the sticky silk glued itself to her forearm.

"You'll get caught yourself," said the hummingbird.

Flory could see that this was a real danger. All the same, she wasn't going to give up. She thought for a moment. "I could cut you loose if I had my dagger," she said. "I have one up in the cherry tree. It's sharp. If you'll wait till I fetch it—"

"No," said the hummingbird. "Listen to me. There may not be time to save me—the spider will poison me soon—but if you would go to my nest and warm the eggs—"

Flory caught her breath. "I could do that!" she exclaimed. "If you tell me where the nest is, I'll go and warm the eggs—and they *won't* die!—and then I'll come back with my dagger and save you."

"Will you?" Something gleamed in the hummingbird's eye. Her throat moved in and out. "Will you save my nestlings?"

"I will," Flory promised. "Tell me where your nest is."

The hummingbird twisted her head, staring hard into Flory's face.

"It's all right," Flory told her. "I don't eat eggs. Ugh."

"I built my nest between the fence post and the wall," whispered the hummingbird, "the fence post close to the fishpond. It's hidden by the barberry bush. You'll have to climb the barberry bush to get to it."

Flory nodded briskly. "I can do that," she said, though she knew how prickly barberry bushes were, and she feared the climb. "Don't worry. I'll find the nest and warm the eggs. And then I'll come back."

She yanked her arm away from the spiderweb. The sticky thread left a red welt on her arm. Flory was not going to fuss over a minor wound like that. She set her teeth, turned her back on the hummingbird, and set forth on her quest.

# The Praying Mantis

As Flory tore though the tall grass, her thoughts flew ahead of her. She knew she must work quickly. She had to fetch her dagger, warm the eggs, and free the hummingbird before the spider came back. When she reached the cherry tree, she flung back her head and bellowed, "Skuggle!"

The cherry leaves shook. Skuggle peered down at her.

"Have you anything to eat?" asked the squirrel.

"No," answered Flory. "Skug, would you

do me a favor? I need to get to my house—quickly."

"Will you give me something to eat?"

Flory rolled her eyes. "No—" she began. Then she changed her mind. "Yes. If you carry me up to my house, I'll give you some dried cherries and sunflower seeds."

The squirrel was at her side before she finished the word *cherries*. "Cherries," he chattered. "I love cherries. You're mean, Flory, to keep them all to yourself. I love them, I want them. Give them to me."

In two seconds they were at the door of Flory's house. "Don't go away," Flory commanded, sliding off the squirrel's tail. "Wait here."

She scrambled into her dim little house. She found her dagger and slipped it into the sash around her waist. Then she picked up the grass quilt she had woven. She rolled it tightly and lashed it to her back.

Skuggle's paws were in the doorway, groping wildly. Flory went to her little store of food and hauled out four dried cherries and five sunflower seeds. One by one, she passed them to the squirrel.

"That's enough," she said, after the fifth seed.

"Don't you have any more?" asked Skuggle.

"Yes, but you can't have them now."

Skuggle's paws went on opening and shutting.

"I said, that's enough," Flory said. "Later."

"But now is when I'm hungry."

Flory was tempted to sting him. "If you take me where I want to go, I'll give you more seeds tomorrow. I'll give you all of them," she said rashly.

"And all the cherries?"

Flory looked over her little stock of food. She had had to lug the sunflower seeds up the tree two by two. The cherries had been even heavier, and it was hard work to pit them. She sighed. "All right. But tomorrow, not today."

"Tomorrow morning?"

"First thing," Flory promised. "Now, get your dirty little mitts out of my house. I'm coming out."

She climbed through the doorway. Skuggle was just outside the house. He nibbled the grass quilt. "Dry," he said sadly, and took another little nip.

"One more bite and I'm going to sting you," warned Flory. "Let me onto your back."

He turned his tail to her. She climbed on and let him flip her to the space behind his ear.

"Where to?"

Flory hesitated. She wanted Skuggle's help, but she didn't want him to get close to the hummingbird's eggs. "The fishpond," she said, after thinking it over. "Hurry!"

The squirrel leaped to the ground. With

dizzying speed he arrived at the edge of the fishpond. Flory gazed into the glassy water. She saw the goldfish gliding below.

"I hear they're good to eat," remarked Skuggle, "but I've never been able to catch any. Raccoon catches them."

Flory felt a pang of fear as she thought of Raccoon. She recalled the thing that no animal and no fairy should ever forget: the world is full of predators. She glanced up at the sky. The blue was dimmer, and the air was growing cool. Soon the bats would come out to hunt. "You can go now," she told Skuggle, but he squatted down next to her, his eyes fixed on the goldfish.

"We might be able to catch 'em if we worked as a team," he said hopefully. "We're a good team, aren't we, Flory? Remember how you used your knife to get the suet out of the grease box? And how I ate it? That was teamwork, wasn't it?"

Flory wanted to scream. She didn't want to

sting Skuggle—she didn't even want to hurt his feelings—but she wanted him to go away. She could see the barberry bush from where she stood. It was going to be a hard climb, and every minute the eggs were getting colder. She dared not begin until Skuggle left. He could whisk up the fence post and gobble the eggs before she climbed to the first branch. She closed her eyes, trying to think of something that would distract him.

The door of the brick house opened. The giantess came out with a jar of seeds. "Look, Skuggle!" Flory cried. "The giantess is going to fill up the seed tube! Hurry up, so you can be the first one there!"

Skuggle bounded to his feet and scampered to the top of the fence. Flory blessed the giantess as she lumbered down the porch steps. Once the seed tube was full, Skuggle would be busy. Then a frightful thought crept into her mind: what if the giantess stopped by the fishpond?

Heavy footsteps shook the ground. Flory crouched down, making herself smaller. The shadow of the giantess passed over her. But the giantess didn't see her. She sauntered past the fishpond, up the stairs, and into the great house.

Once the door closed, Flory breathed a sigh of relief. "Now for the barberry bush," she said, and sprang to her feet.

The climb took all her skill. The barberry bush was leathery and tough, with purple leaves and cruel thorns. One of the thorns raked Flory's forearm, leaving a long, painful scratch. Flory stopped to lick the blood away. Then she looked up.

Her heart stood still. A praying mantis squatted in the barberry bush. He was less than four inches from the nest. As Flory gaped at him, his antennae twitched. He turned his head as if he knew she was there. His head was triangular, with bulging green eyes on the sides.

Flory went cold. She knew how dangerous he was—how suddenly he could strike. She also knew what was in store if he caught her. His spiky forelegs would dig into her flesh. The mantis would lift her to his bristled mouth and bite through her neck. Then he would eat her body, saving her head for last.

She opened her mouth to say her stinging spell. Then she shut it. If she stung him, he would dart away from her—closer to the nest. She wondered whether he was climbing toward the eggs or away from them. She wished she could work her seeing spell and find out if the nest was empty or full, but she dared not close her eyes.

"Night fairy," hissed the mantis, "where are your wings?"

The word *wings* gave Flory an idea. She backed up against a thorny branch. "My wings!"

Her voice was high and panicky. "Help me! I've ripped my wings on the thorns! I can't fly!"

It worked. The mantis turned his long body toward her. He was eager for easy prey. Flory wanted to flee; he was a dreadful thing, and her skin crawled as he came closer. But with every step he took, he was farther from the nest.

"Night fairy!" His voice was as soft as a lullaby. "Night fairy, will you be my prey?"

His huge green eyes seemed to be casting a spell over her. He swayed back and forth. In spite of herself, Flory began to sway with him.

All at once, he struck. His spiked legs sliced the air. Flory sprang to one side and shrieked her stinging spell. Never before had she stung so hard. The mantis's body jerked.

"Go!" shouted Flory. "Go, or I'll sting again!"

The mantis's eyes were full of hatred. He lurched back as if to attack. Flory drew her dagger. Instead of leaping backward, she

threw herself forward, under his forelegs. She slashed upward, missing his throat by a hair. The double attack—dagger and sting—was too much for the insect. He spread his wings and flew away.

Flory watched until he was out of sight. In spite of her victory, her heart was sick. She was afraid she had come too late—that the eggs had been eaten or grown too cold. Nevertheless, she sheathed her dagger and began the last part of the climb.

The nest above her was the size of a walnut shell. The hummingbird had woven it from dry cobwebs and covered the outside with lichen, so that it blended in with the old wooden fence. Flory caught hold of the edge with her hands, hooked one ankle over the rim, and slid down inside.

The eggs were still there. Two of them, as white as pearls. When Flory touched them, she knew at once that they were too cold. They ought to have been warmer. But the creatures inside were alive. She could feel them, curled tight inside the shells: one male, one female. As she spread her fingers over the shells, she felt a glow of triumph and something else, something strong and sweet and steady. She had saved the unborn birds from the praying mantis. Now she would save them from the cold.

She pressed her palms flat against the shells and began to sing. She sang a spell of comfort for small living things. As she sang, she thought of the warmest things she knew: strong sunlight on black stone, heat lightning on summer nights, the candles that the giantess burned on the patio table. The heat of her thoughts surged through her hands. She could feel the unhatched birds yearning for it.

By the time she finished singing, the two little eggs hummed with life. Flory pushed them together and tucked the grass quilt over them. "Now," she said, "you must stay warm until your mother comes home." She stooped down and kissed the quilt twice. "I'm going to bring her home soon," she added, "but you'll be warm through the night."

She felt to make sure her dagger was still at her side. Then she wrapped both hands around the nearest barberry twig, kicked off from the nest, and swung herself down through the branches.

It was later than she thought. Night would come soon.

Chapter Eight
# *The Spider*

Never had the garden seemed so large. Flory's legs were scratched and aching, and the rough brick of the patio scraped the soles of her feet. Nevertheless, she set a good pace, sprinting and leaping over the cracks between the bricks.

It was growing dark. A pale star winked in the sky, and the colors of the garden were fading. The white roses glowed in the dimness like the star overhead. By the time Flory reached the juniper bush, she had a stitch in her side, but her footsteps never slowed. She must cut the web and free the hummingbird before the bats came out to hunt.

She had forgotten about the spider. While Flory had been warming the eggs, the spider had returned and found the hummingbird trapped in its web. Now the spider was wrapping its prey, creeping around and around the open wings, wet silk dripping from its spinnerets.

Flory stood stock-still, gazing upward. The spider was a large creature—a female, no doubt, as male spiders are puny. Her black-and-yellow body was as long as Flory was tall, and a good deal fatter. She was beautiful, in a scary, black-and-yellow sort of way, but she was deadly. Flory thought of the spider's fangs digging into her and shivered. Nevertheless, she spat on her hands and caught hold of the bottom strand of the spiderweb.

The spider's head jerked up. Although she had eight eyes, her eyesight was poor.

She couldn't see Flory, but she felt the web move under the fairy's weight. The spider swung downward, hanging from a thread. She grumbled something that sounded like "feast or famine" and "always the way." The hairy forelegs twitched, testing the air. "Why, it's a fairy!" cried the spider. "What's a fairy doing in my web? Are you stuck?"

She did not sound unfriendly. It took Flory a moment to gather her thoughts. "I'm not stuck," she answered. She took care to speak more politely than usual; she had an idea that spiders must be treated with respect. "I came to free the hummingbird. Don't you think she's a bit big for you to eat?"

"I can eat her," said the spider. "I've never caught anything I couldn't eat. For that matter, I could eat you." She gave a low chuckle. "Mind you, I don't want to. They say it's bad luck to kill a fairy, and I don't fancy bad luck. But I could eat you, missy—if I wanted to."

Flory didn't doubt it. Seeing the spider up close, she was tempted to leap down from the web and shriek for Skuggle. She cast a nervous glance at the hummingbird. The bird hung limp, eyes closed. "You've poisoned her!" Flory said accusingly.

"Not yet," answered the spider. "I like to wrap 'em before I bite 'em. That way you don't waste so much juice."

Flory's thoughts raced. If the hummingbird hadn't been bitten yet, there was still hope. "If you haven't bitten her, why isn't she moving?"

"She's gone into torpor," the spider explained. "Hummingbirds do that. When they run out of strength, they slow their bodies down. That's why she looks dead—but she's not. A good thing, too. I don't like dead meat. I like it hot and juicy." She nodded toward a grayish bundle on the other side of the web. "Take that wasp. He's still alive and kicking. What I say is, a dead wasp is nasty, but—"

Flory forgot about being polite. "Why not eat the wasp?" she interrupted. "You don't need a whole big bird to eat. Why don't you eat the wasp and let the hummingbird go?"

The spider looked affronted. "Who do you think you are?" she asked. "Telling me what to eat! I'll eat what I choose, missy! It's no business of yours."

"It is my business," Flory said rashly. "The hummingbird's my friend. If you try to bite her, I'll sting you. And I'll stick you with my dagger." She drew her knife and brandished it fiercely. "Let her go!"

The spider's eyes gleamed faintly red. All at once, she swung downward, heading for Flory. The black-and-yellow legs swung into action, moving with incredible speed.

Flory panicked. She shouted her stinging spell so fast that she mixed up the magic words. The spider danced closer. Flory closed her eyes. She thought of the spell she used when making cobweb ropes. She imagined a vine spiraling toward the sun, twisting, twisting. The words spilled from her lips.

When she opened her eyes, she saw that the spell had worked. The threads of the cobweb had coiled tightly, snagging the spider in her own web. Ropes of silk fettered the black-and-yellow body. Sticky threads gummed the spider's mouth shut. Three of the eight legs were folded under themselves. The other five stuck out at queer angles, twitching helplessly.

Flory gave a little gasp. She wasn't sorry that her spell had worked, but it was clear that the spider was in great pain. It was also clear that Flory had made an enemy. The spider's eyes bulged with rage.

"I didn't mean it." Flory said hastily. "I mean, I meant it, but—" Her voice trailed off as she eyed the spider's left foreleg. It was so bent and crooked that it made Flory feel a little sick. "Here—hold still. That leg's going to snap in two if I don't—Hold still, I say! I'm going to cut the ties."

She clenched the knife and darted forward, nicking the thread that held the spider's leg. The leg shuddered back into place.

"There!" Flory said nervously. "Is that better?"

The spider glared at her. Flory hesitated. Then she switched her knife to her other hand so that she could wipe her sweaty palm on her skirt. Her heart beat fast as she cut the threads that bound the other seven legs. When she finished, the spider was still her prisoner, but the eight legs hung straight and free, like the petals of a black daisy.

"Now!" Flory said briskly. "Don't you feel better?"

The spider flexed her legs, making sure they still worked. Her eyes were still furious, but it was clear that she was no longer in agony.

"I have an idea," Flory announced. "I'd like

to cut the threads around your mouth so that we can talk things over. Only you mustn't bite me. Promise me you won't bite me."

There was no answer. Flory took a deep breath. Then she wedged the blade of her knife under the threads around the spider's jaw. She tried to keep her hands as far from the great fangs as she could, but she couldn't cut the cords without getting close. The spider's fangs were sharply pointed and curved inward, like the horns of a bull. Flory knew that the poison inside those fangs was powerful enough to turn her bones and muscles to soup. Her stomach felt queasy with terror, but her hand did not shake. She sawed carefully until she cut the thread from the spider's jaw.

The spider opened her mouth and said a long string of bad words.

Flory couldn't blame her. She waited until the spider had run out of things to say. Then she said, "Here's my idea." She pointed to the web, which was dotted with little gray bundles. "You have other good things to eat in your web. If you promise not to eat the hummingbird, I'll set you free."

"Why shouldn't I eat the hummingbird?" demanded the spider. "Isn't she my prey? Didn't I work to weave the web that caught her? Don't I have to eat?"

Flory's hand dropped to her side. It was true what the spider said: every creature in the garden had to eat. That was the law. The spider had only been obeying it. But—

"You could eat wasps," Flory said stubbornly. "Promise not to eat the bird, and I'll set you free."

The spider scowled. "What if I won't?"

"Then you starve to death," Flory said unkindly. She put her hands on her hips. "I can sting you. And I can tie you up. So you have to do what I say."

The spider shook herself, straining against

the ropes around her belly. "I'm not promising anything unless you say you're sorry."

It was Flory's turn to scowl. She had never said she was sorry in her life. She didn't like the idea of saying it. "I won't," she said. "Besides, I'm cutting you free. You ought to be grateful."

"I'm not free yet," answered the spider, "and I'm not grateful."

Flory stamped her foot. "I'm not asking you to starve," she said irritably. "All I'm asking is for you not to eat the hummingbird." After a minute she added, "Or me."

"And all I'm asking is for you to say you're sorry," retorted the spider. "You hurt my legs and you hurt my pride. So you have to say sorry, and"—a glint of malice lit her eyes—"you have to say it right."

Flory laid her hand on the hilt of her dagger. "What do you mean, 'say it right?'"

"I mean you have to mean it," the spider said. "If you don't say you're sorry, I'd rather stay here and starve. I *will* starve, and it will be all your fault."

Flory made an angry little noise in the back of her throat. This was all taking too long. The spider was her prisoner, and prisoners shouldn't tell their jailors what to do. All the same, Flory knew she had met her match. The spider was as stubborn as she was. She shut her eyes and tried to imagine being sorry. It was hard work, almost like casting a spell.

She imagined that she was a spider, a proud and dangerous spider. She imagined what it was like to spin an elegant web, only to be caught in it herself. She imagined having eight legs and having them twisted and trapped and hurt. After a moment, she bit her lip.

"I'm sorry," she said in a low voice.

"That'll do," said the spider. "Cut me free."

Flory stuck her dagger back in her sash. "You haven't promised not to eat the hummingbird."

"I promise," answered the spider. She gave a low chuckle. "Truth is, I don't like raw bird very much—but I hate the way birds leave a big hole in my web. I ought to give her"—she jerked one leg to point at the hummingbird—"a pinch and a poison, just for making such a mess! But when all is said and done, I hate wasps more than birds. There's things I could tell you about wasps that would make your blood run cold."

Flory thought that her blood had run cold enough for one evening. She said, "I'll try to free the bird without cutting your web too much."

"Hmmmph." The spider tapped the web with one oily foot. "That's good of you. But if I were you, I wouldn't cut her loose just yet. Wait until dawn."

"Why?"

"Look at her." The spider shook herself,

freed at last. "She's still in torpor. If you cut her loose, she'll fall. She's safer in the web than on the ground."

"But I have to cut her loose. She has to go home." Flory raised her eyes to the unmoving bird. "How do I wake her up?"

"You can't," said the spider. "That's the thing about torpor. She won't come out of it till the sun rises and she warms up."

"But she has to fly *now*," Flory said. "She has to go back to her nest, and I have to go home."

"She's not going anywhere tonight," said the spider.

Flory's heart sank. Night had almost fallen. The green plants looked gray, and the stars were brightening. At any moment, the bats would leave their hollow in the oak tree. It was time to take shelter in her safe little home—but if she left, the hummingbird would be food for any animal that found her.

Flory said slowly, "I can't stay here and guard her—"

"Nobody asked you to," said the spider. "What I say is, every creature has to take care of herself."

Flory agreed. She had taken care of herself ever since she was three days old. She thought of her lily-leaf hammock and how tired and scratched and sore she felt. Then she remembered the baby hummingbirds. She had kissed them and promised them that their mother would come back.

"Oh, all right!" she said furiously. "I'll stay."

"Suit yourself," said the spider. "I'm going to eat that wasp. Do you want a piece?"

"No, I don't," Flory said firmly. "I don't like wasps—not even to eat."

The spider began to pick her way up the web. She turned back. "If you're going to spend the night in the web, you should know that the cross-threads are the sticky ones."

"Thank you," said Flory. She meant it.

The spider shinnied away. Flory was left alone. She climbed up the juniper bush and settled down close to the hummingbird. A dog barked in the distance. Flory had an odd sense that something was missing. Then she knew what it was. The birds had stopped singing. They were roosting for the night instead of leaping from branch to branch.

Suddenly the night was alive with shrill sounds. It was the moment Flory had been dreading. She gripped the juniper twig until her fingers ached. She heard leathery wings beating the air and saw the jagged shapes of bats against the sky. But they did not come looking for her. Bats hunt in the air, not close to the ground.

Once they had flown away, Flory began to breathe again. She caught a glimpse of gleaming white between the trees. The moon was rising—the beautiful moon. Its light did

not dazzle her or make her eyes water. She could look at it as long as she liked.

A tiny green light appeared above the grass. Then another. The lightning bugs were rising. One by one they lit their lamps and floated toward the sky. Flory gazed at them, rapt. All at once she realized how homesick she had been for the night. She was not sleepy. She had been up since dawn, but she knew that she would have no trouble staying awake. She was, after all, a night fairy. This was her time.

Chapter Nine

*The Raccoon*

Hours passed. Flory swung back and forth on the juniper twig and gazed at the moon. The night breeze tickled her sweetly. The fireflies blinked on and off, now green, now golden. From time to time, Flory heard the faint *shhhh* of the grass moving and saw long shadows cross the ground. The earthworms were leaving their burrows, coming out to breathe the moist air.

A curious chuckling sound caught her attention. Flory held her breath.

A raccoon was drinking from the fishpond. She could hear his tongue as he lapped the water. Noiselessly, Flory got to her feet and peered through the darkness. She saw the grizzled hump of the raccoon's body. He was combing the water, searching for goldfish. Flory prayed that he would catch one and eat his fill, but her hopes were dashed. He looked up, eyes gleaming, nostrils twitching. She could almost feel him smelling her.

He came straight toward the juniper bush, his claws making a faint *click-click* on the patio. His eyes flashed yellow in the dark. Now he was close enough that Flory could see his dark mask and the weird prettiness of his face. "Who's there?" he barked.

Flory didn't move a muscle.

The raccoon came closer. The long, ringed tail swung over the grass like a fat snake. Flory gritted her teeth, clenched her fists, and stung.

The raccoon stopped in his tracks. "Ow,"

he said in an annoyed tone of voice. "What are you?"

"I'm a night fairy," Flory said with dignity.

The raccoon opened his jaws, licking the roof of his mouth as if he tasted something bitter. "I don't eat fairies," the raccoon said. "I ate one once, and it stung me. It didn't taste very good."

"Then you'd better leave me alone," said Flory. "I sting *very* hard. I practice a lot."

"All right. I won't eat you," the raccoon answered glibly. He sniffed again. "I smell something good to eat. Is it bird?"

Flory's hand stole to the hilt of her knife. "You'd better go away." She knew that her words, like her threats, were idle. The raccoon was huge, sleek, and muscular. If he made up his mind that he wanted the hummingbird, she would not be able to stop him.

The raccoon chuckled. He had seen

the bird. His claw shot out and nabbed the hummingbird, snapping the threads of the spiderweb. Flory stung as hard as she could.

The raccoon gave a little yip. He dropped the bird and put his paw in his mouth. "Would you stop *doing* that?" He licked the bottom of his paw. "Oof. I hate cobwebs." His tongue swept the edges of his mouth. Then he bent down and picked up the hummingbird in his jaws.

"Let go!" screamed Flory. She grabbed a thread of the spiderweb and swung to the ground. She yanked her hand free, so angry that she didn't feel it when the web ripped off a layer of skin. "You stop! Let go of that bird, or I'll stab you!"

The raccoon cocked his head. He loomed over her, and his bright eyes twinkled. He was ten times as big as Skuggle and thirty times as heavy. But Flory was too furious to care.

She darted forward and slashed the raccoon's forepaw with her dagger. When she pulled the knife free, there was blood on the tip.

"Stop that!" snarled the raccoon, shaking his paw. Flory thrust again. This time she missed.

"Silly fairy," said the raccoon, "You can't fight me! Leave me alone, or I'll have to hurt you!"

"I won't!" screamed Flory. "Go away, or I'll kill you!"

The raccoon laughed so hard that the hummingbird fell out of his mouth. Flory slashed at him with her knife. This time the raccoon struck back, smacking her with such force that she tumbled headlong over the grass. Flory sat up and uttered her stinging spell. She was amazed by her own strength. The raccoon winced as she stung again. Her spells were small wounds, mere pinpricks under the raccoon's fur. But it was Flory's time, a little before midnight, and her magic was at its strongest. Though the stings were small ones, they came one after another, pelting the raccoon from all sides.

The raccoon was losing patience. He had been stung all over his body, and the pad of his front paw was bleeding. He lowered his head and crouched down, growling.

A bat squeaked. The cry of a bat is a common sound at night, and the raccoon paid no attention. But Flory threw down her dagger and covered her head with her arms.

The bat streaked toward them, coming within an inch of the raccoon's head. The raccoon ducked, and the bat zigzagged back. His mouth was open, showing needle-sharp teeth. The skin wings jerked and rippled. No sight could have been more terrifying to Flory. She burrowed into the grass.

The bat's squeaks grew softer, then louder—Flory felt the wind of his wings—then

softer again. When Flory dared to raise her head, she saw that the raccoon had scampered a few feet away. He sat back on his haunches, a baffled look on his face.

Little brown bats are insect eaters. They do not attack raccoons. But the bat swooped down again, shrieking curses.

Flory began to understand that he was not after her. He was tormenting the raccoon. She watched as he drove the raccoon across the patio and past the fishpond. The raccoon dodged and ducked, spinning in circles, but the bat would not leave him alone. At last the raccoon slunk under the garden fence. The ringed tail vanished.

The bat chittered with triumph and circled back toward Flory. He flopped down on the grass less than six inches away. Flory was so frightened that tears filled her eyes.

"Don't cry," the bat said gently. "Don't you see? I came to help."

Flory's mouth was too dry to utter a spell. Her hand went to her side, seeking her dagger.

"Your knife's by your left foot," the bat told her. "Only please don't stab me. Or sting me. I don't blame you for wanting to, but please don't."

Flory picked up her dagger and got to her feet. She stared at the bat.

He was really rather a small bat. His wingspan was huge—like two large pinecones set end to end—but now that he was close to her, she could see that he wasn't much bigger than she was. He was mouse-size, with a pushed-in snout and enormous ears that were set wide apart, like moths' wings. He lay belly-flopped on the ground with his elbows folded up like jackknives.

Flory's voice shook. "What do you want?"

"Well," said the bat, "I don't want to hurt you. Or your friend." He nodded toward the hummingbird in the grass. "How did you come to make friends with a hummingbird? They're not friendly birds, you know."

"I know," Flory said with feeling. She thought a moment. "We're not really friends. I was hoping she would let me ride on her back one day."

The bat opened his mouth as if he wanted to say something. But Flory went on speaking. "That's how it started. The first time I saw a hummingbird, I knew I wanted to ride on one. I didn't care whether they were friendly or not. I just liked the way they looked."

"Who doesn't?" said the bat. "They're beautiful birds. Amazing fliers. Of course, bats are good fliers, too—" He paused, once again as if there was something he wanted to say. But Flory interrupted.

"I hate bats," she said.

"I know," said the bat humbly. "It's my fault."

Flory gasped. "It was you?"

"I was younger then," the bat said pleadingly. "Try to understand. I was asleep for the winter—I'd found a nice little attic for my home. Then one night, the door opened and the giants charged in. They had bright lights in their hands, and they were shouting—you'd think they were afraid of us! Luckily I got away through a hole in the roof. But of course, it was early for me to be out, and I was half-asleep and terribly hungry. I saw you and I thought you were a luna moth. I ought to have known better—luna moths in April!—but I wasn't thinking clearly."

"I see," Flory said slowly.

"I've been sorry ever since," the bat went on. "And I've wanted to tell you so. I looked for you night after night—I thought you must have dropped down close to this garden—and I called out to you, but no one ever answered. Then tonight I heard a fairy screaming. I came closer, and I listened for the echoes, and I heard that the fairy's wings were jagged and torn. That's when I knew it was you."

"Oh," said Flory. She thought of all the nights she had huddled inside the cedar house with cobwebs in her ears, trying to block out the sounds of the bats.

"There's one thing more," the bat added. He sounded nervous. "I know I'm not a hummingbird—and your wings are coming along nicely—but if—"

Flory held up her hand. "Wait. Stop. What do you mean, my wings are coming along nicely? What do you *mean*?"

The bat raised himself up on his elbows. "I mean they're growing back," he said. "I can hear them. Can't you?"

Flory shook her head. She reached behind her, feeling up and down the ruffle of wings on her spine. The scabs had fallen away; she had known that. She couldn't tell if the wings felt longer or not. She craned her neck, trying to see over her shoulder.

"Oh, my dear," the bat said softly. "Didn't you know? Your wings will grow back as your magic grows stronger. They've already begun. I don't see very well—but I can hear the cells growing, if I listen carefully. Can't you?"

"No," answered Flory. "I can't hear that well. And I can't see behind me."

"They're growing," the bat told her. He gave a little shriek, and his huge ears rippled. "I can *hear* the echo. You can make mistakes with your eyes, but ears never lie. At least, my ears don't."

Flory wanted to dance and weep for joy. "Then—I'll have wings again!" She saw herself flying through the garden on her own wings, dipping through the spray of the fountain, soaring over the snapdragons. "I'll be able to fly!"

"Yes," agreed the bat. "And in the meantime"—he sounded suddenly shy—"if you want someone to fly you around, well, there's me. I'd be happy to carry you. Of course, I'm not as beautiful as a hummingbird—most creatures think bats are rather ugly—but I'd like to help, because, you see, I am so very sorry."

Flory thought about what the bat was saying. She looked at him, with his long, clever fingers and the soft fur around his face. He wasn't glittering and magical like the hummingbird, but Flory liked his face. It was a gentle face, and she felt that she could trust him.

"I don't think you're ugly," she told him. "What's your name?"

## Chapter Ten

# *Homecoming*

His name was Peregrine, which means
"traveler." Flory told him her name meant
"flower," and all at once they were friends.

They passed the rest of the night together,
guarding the hummingbird. Together they
freed the bird from the spider's silk. Flory
used the flat edge of her dagger to drag the
cords off the feathers, and Peregrine used
the thumbnails on the edges of his wings.
When the threads clung together, Peregrine
bit through them with his sharp teeth.

"After we finish taking off the web, I could take you for a ride," Peregrine hinted, but Flory refused.

"I have to keep watch over the hummingbird," she explained. "I promised." She hadn't really promised, but she felt as if she had. Peregrine looked so crestfallen that she added quickly, "But I'd like to go tomorrow night."

"I could take you back home," Peregrine said. "We could go north, where the woods are, and find other night fairies."

Flory's eyes lit up. She had almost forgotten what it was like to live among other fairies. Then she thought of her little cedar house, and the hummingbird's eggs hatching and Skuggle.

"I'd like to go back sometime," she told Peregrine. "But I don't think that's my home anymore. I think my home is here." And because the bat, with his huge leathery ears, was a good listener, she told him all about becoming a day fairy and the home she had made for herself.

"Do you think you'll go on being a day fairy?"

Flory shook her head. "No. But I won't live only at night, either. I like night best, but daytime is good, too. I like the way the flowers look when they're awake. I like the colors and the birds. . . . Not all the birds are safe, but I like to watch them." She lowered her voice. "And I like Skuggle. He's a squirrel, but I like him anyway."

She looked at Peregrine to see if he was surprised, but his beady black eyes were shut and he was yawning. The sky was turning gray. It was time for him to go back to his hollow in the oak tree.

"Perry," she said softly. "Wake up. It's time to roost."

The bat gave himself a little shake. "I'm sorry. I must have dozed off."

"It's time for you to go home," Flory said

firmly. "It's nearly dawn. Aren't you sleepy?"

Peregrine yawned again. "Not that sleepy," he said bravely.

"Yes, you are," Flory told him. "You're a *bat*. So go home. I'll stay with the hummingbird. It won't be long before she wakes up—and I'm not frightened. Now that I'm not afraid of you, I'm not afraid of anything." She put out her hand and gave him a little shove. "Go on."

Peregrine flapped his wings and swerved toward the sky. Flory watched him disappear into the oak leaves.

The grass was wet with dew. In a little while, the sun would rise. Flory's eyelids felt crusty, and she rubbed her eyes with her fists. When she caught herself nodding, she got to her feet and circled the hummingbird, her hand on the hilt of her dagger.

The hummingbird stirred. The branches were rustling now, and the birds were beginning their early-morning chorus. From time to time, the hummingbird shifted. She was coming out of her torpor.

Flory went to the bird's head so that they could see eye to eye. "Hummingbird, I'm here," she crooned. "Are you awake yet? I put a spell on your eggs. They're still warm—I'm almost sure of it."

As if in answer, the hummingbird rose into the air. She flew straight to the water tube without looking back. Flory watched as she drank. "Birds," she said bitterly. She thought of all she had done for the hummingbird's sake, and she wanted to shout over the unfairness of it all.

But she was too weary to shout, and she had a long walk ahead of her. She trudged back toward the cherry tree, head drooping. Then she heard the whirr of wings.

The hummingbird perched on a clover stalk in front of her. "Come!" said the bird.

"Come where?" asked Flory.

"To the nest," answered the hummingbird, as if Flory had asked a stupid question. She flicked her wings impatiently. "Hurry up and climb on my back. I want to see my little ones."

"But you said—"

"I said I wouldn't be your slave and carry you wherever you wanted," the hummingbird answered sharply. "This is different. Come along—you've earned it. Climb on my back."

Flory didn't need to be asked again. She shoved her dagger in her sash and scrambled up the shining feathers. The hummingbird was surprisingly slippery. Flory folded her legs tightly around the bird's neck. She wished there were something to hold on to.

The green grass fell away. At close range, the whirr of the wings was like the racket of a waterfall. The flight was glorious but nerve-wracking; the bird dodged and veered so

sharply that Flory shrieked. But Flory liked it. She had no doubt about that.

All too soon they reached the nest. "What's this?" asked the hummingbird. Her beak bobbed down and pinched Flory's quilt.

"It's mine—" Flory began. "I thought it would keep—Oh!"

Under the quilt were two tiny birds. They had shiny black skin and no feathers; they were wrinkled and skinny, and their tiny beaks were like needles. They were very ugly. Flory loved them at first sight.

The hummingbird plunged her beak into one open mouth. Her stomach jerked in and out as she forced the sugar water she had drunk into the baby bird. Then she turned to the second nestling and fed him. Flory sat on the edge of the nest and watched. She felt a little shy.

"They're—" She stopped. No one could

call the baby hummingbirds beautiful. "I like them," she said.

"Of course you like them," the hummingbird said smugly. "They're the most beautiful children you ever saw."

Flory put her hand to her mouth to hide a smile. She was just in time to cover a yawn.

"I suppose you're sleepy," the hummingbird said. "You're a night fairy, after all. I'm going out for more sugar water. Do you want another ride?"

"Yes," Flory said happily. She thought about her little house and the heavenly softness of her hammock. "Please take me home."

Her home was tidy and peaceful. Flory crawled through the door hole and stumbled over to the hammock. It had been a long day and a long night. She was covered with scratches, and her poppy-red dress was shredded so that she

would never be able to mend it. All the same, she was very happy. She felt that she had never been so happy in her life.

She tore off her dress and climbed into the hammock. Tonight, Peregrine would come and carry her away. She wondered what his flight would be like. She looked forward to finding out. Bats fly high; she would swoop over the garden, close to the moon and the stars. . . . Her eyes closed. She was falling sweetly into sleep.

There was a scratching sound outside the door. Flory ignored it. But the noise grew louder, and at last she was forced to open her eyes. The light from the doorway was almost blotted out by two twitching paws.

"You promised me cherries," said Skuggle.

🦋 LAURA AMY SCHLITZ is the author of the 2008 Newbery Medal–winning book, *Good Masters! Sweet Ladies! Voices from a Medieval Village,* illustrated by Robert Byrd. In addition to that much-honored and highly praised collection, her credits include *A Drowned Maiden's Hair: A Melodrama,* the recipient of the inaugural Cybils Award for a middle-grade novel, as well as many other honors and accolades. Those two titles and her biography, *The Hero Schliemann: The Dreamer Who Dug for Troy,* illustrated by Robert Byrd, were all Junior Library Guild Selections. Laura Amy Schlitz's retelling of a Grimm fairy tale, *The Bearskinner,* illustrated by Max Grafe, was named an American Library Association Notable Children's Book and a *Horn Book* Fanfare selection.

Making a journey into the world of fairy in order to write about the night fairy, Flory, came naturally to Laura Amy Schlitz. "As a child," she explains, "I adored fairies and fairy tales." She was also motivated by the girls who came into the library where she works, seeking books about fairies. "They adore the prettiness of fairies, the miniature-ness," she says, "but they are also nature lovers and lovers of adventure. They are in fact quite interesting little girls—the future wild women of America. I couldn't help thinking that these little girls who love fairies deserve something lively."

Laura Amy Schlitz has spent most of her life working as a librarian and a professional storyteller. She has also written plays for young people that have been performed in professional theaters all over the country. She lives in Baltimore, where she is currently lower-school librarian at the Park School.

ANGELA BARRETT studied at the Royal College of Art in England with Quentin Blake and is one of Britain's most highly acclaimed illustrators. She has won the Nestlé Smarties Book Prize and the W. H. Smith Illustration Award for her work and has illustrated more than twenty-four books for children, including many classic tales and fairy tales, biographies, story collections, and picture books. Among her many titles are *Beauty and the Beast,* retold by Max Eilenberg; *The Emperor's New Clothes,* retold by Naomi Lewis; *Through the Tempests Dark and Wild: A Story of Mary Shelley, Creator of Frankenstein* by Sharon Darrow; *Rocking Horse Land and Other Tales of Dolls and Toys,* compiled by Naomi Lewis; and *Joan of Arc* and *Anne Frank,* both by Josephine Poole.

"When I was young," she recounts, "creating miniature worlds was a favorite thought before going to sleep. If Flory had had a less exciting life, I would have enjoyed drawing a very detailed domestic interior for her. But she is a creature of simple needs, and after providing herself with a bed, clothes, and storage under difficult circumstances, she gets on with her mission outdoors. She is brave and resourceful—a perfect heroine."

Angela Barrett lives in London, where she illustrates full-time.

# Praise for *The Night Fairy*

"For years, I've been searching for a new Harry Potter contender, and every year I've come up short. But an answer has come in an unlikely form . . . a glowing novel called *The Night Fairy*. . . . Out of Flory's longing to fly arise several hair-raising adventures, in which she must risk her life, tangle with deadly creatures, and prove both her bravery and magical ability. . . . Schlitz has gone beyond a girl's or boy's book into the best realm of fantasy, where character, adventure, nature, challenge, and mystery all meet in one radiant place." —*Boston Globe*

"In ways that will delight readers, Flory works out how to feed and clothe herself. For protection, she fashions a thorn into a sword; for transportation, she enlists the services of a perpetually hungry squirrel. . . . *The Night Fairy* has the effect of making readers feel as if they've crept through a magic portal into a fairy-scale world." —*Wall Street Journal*

★ "A far cry from the conventionally sweet stories about fairies, this tale begins with violence and ends with redemption. In between is an imaginative adventure story in a familiar, yet exotic landscape. . . . This finely crafted and unusually dynamic fairy story is a natural for reading aloud."

—*Booklist* (starred review)

★ "Flory struggles at first with . . . creatures that do not look at the world the same way she does. She quickly learns that kindness, compassion, generosity, and bravery can help her to make much-needed friends. Written in short chapters, this beautifully crafted tale works equally well as a read-aloud or as independent reading. . . . Sure to be a favorite among girls who love fairies." —*School Library Journal* (starred review)

"A whimsical and cozy tale. . . . The story reveals how handicaps can be overcome through quick thinking and determination."
—*Publishers Weekly*

"Schlitz explores Flory's moral development, magical spells, and cleverness as she learns to wield a dagger with a vengeance, sting predators with her mind, and make friends with squirrels and hummingbirds. . . . . Fans of Dahl's *Minipins,* Huygen's *Gnomes,* and Cannon's *Stellaluna* will enjoy Flory's wit and derring-do." —*The Horn Book*

"Schlitz creates pure magic in her depiction of Flory's world, deftly blending the appealing sweetness of the more popular portrayals of fairies with the darkly subversive, but still subtle, tone of traditional folklore. . . . Presents an intriguing picture of the secret workings of nature. . . . Brings both the gossamer lightness of fairy stories and the rich darkness of fantasy to its tale, and readers will revel in Flory's mysterious and sometimes magical realm." —*Bulletin of the Center for Children's Books*

**Also by Laura Amy Schlitz**

*The Bearskinner: A Tale of the Brothers Grimm*
illustrated by Max Grafe

*A Drowned Maiden's Hair: A Melodrama*

*Good Masters! Sweet Ladies!*
*Voices from a Medieval Village*
illustrated by Robert Byrd

*The Hero Schliemann:*
*The Dreamer Who Dug for Troy*
illustrated by Robert Byrd